DATE DUE			

6788

FIC   Mattern, Joanne.

Kidnapped.

KIDNAPPED

Library of Congress Cataloging-in-Publication Data

Mattern, Joanne, (date)
    Kidnapped / by Robert Louis Stevenson; retold by Joanne Mattern;
illustrated by Steve Parton.
        p.   cm. (Troll illustrated classics)
    Summary: After being kidnapped by his villainous uncle, sixteen-
year-old David Balfour escapes and becomes involved in the struggle
of the Scottish highlanders against English rule.
    ISBN 0-8167-2862-3 (lib. bdg.)   ISBN 0-8167-2863-1 (pbk.)
    [1. Scotland—History—18th century—Fiction.   2. Adventure and
adventurers—Fiction.]   I. Parton, Steven, ill.   II. Stevenson,
Robert Louis, 1850-1894. Kidnapped.   III. Title.
PZ7.M43165Ki 1993
[Fic]—dc20   92-5803

KIDNAPPED

ROBERT LOUIS STEVENSON

Retold by
Joanne Mattern

Illustrated by
Steve Parton

Troll Associates

I will begin the story of my adventures with a morning in the month of June, in the year 1751, when I left my father's house for the last time. The sun was just beginning to shine over the hills as I went down the road, and the birds were singing in the trees.

Mr. Campbell, the minister of Essendean, was waiting for me by the garden gate. "Davie, lad," he said, "I will walk with you for a while."

We walked along for a bit in silence. Then Mr. Campbell asked, "Are you sorry to leave Essendean?"

"Well, sir," I said, "it is hard for me to answer your question. I have been happy here, but now that my father and mother are both dead, there is nothing left for me here. Still, if I knew where I was going and what awaited me there, I would be happier about leaving."

"Very well, Davie," Mr. Campbell said. "I will tell you your future, or at least what part of it I can. Before your father died, he gave me a letter for you. You're to take it to the house of Shaws, not far from here. 'That is the place I came from,' your father said, 'and it is where my boy should return.'"

"The house of Shaws!" I cried, for I knew that was a great house indeed. "What had my father to do with that?"

"It is where you are from, Davie, for you are David Balfour of Shaws." He gave me the letter then, and I stared at it in wonder. "To the hands of Ebenezer Balfour, Esquire, of Shaws," it said, "this is delivered by my son, David Balfour." I could hardly believe that I, a poor country lad, only seventeen years old, had such a great future before me. "Should I go?" I asked Mr. Campbell, suddenly afraid.

"Of course," said the minister. "It is only two days' walk there. If the worst happens, and your fine relations do not want you, you can always come back and knock at my door. You know I will do my best for you. But I would rather see you set out upon the path your father meant for you."

He was right, of course, so I said good-bye to him. There were tears on his face, and I know there should have been on mine as well. But I was so excited at the adventure that lay before me, and at going to live in a fine house, that I could not help but be happy to start out on my journey.

Just before noon on the second day, I came to the top of a hill. Looking down, I saw the country fall away before me, down to the sea. I had never set eyes on the sea before. It was a beautiful sight, especially since I knew I was near the house of Shaws, my new home.

I had to ask for directions to the house, and the replies I received took some of the joy out of me. My questions seemed to surprise the village folk, and they looked at me uneasily, as if they did not like to think of the house of Shaws.

"Is it a great house?" I asked one man who was pulling a cart down the lane.

"I'm sure," he said. "It is very big."

"And the people in it?"

"People?" he said sharply. "There are no people there."

"Not even Mr. Ebenezer?" I asked, puzzled.

"Oh, yes, he is there, if that's who you're wanting." He shook his head. "It's none of my business, laddie, but if I were you, I would stay away from Mr. Ebenezer and the house of Shaws."

Other folk I met told me much the same thing. I began to wonder what kind of place I was going to, that everyone seemed startled and afraid at the very mention of it. And what sort of man was Mr. Ebenezer? I was almost tempted to walk back to Essendean, so worried was I at what awaited me. But I had come so far already, and my father had wanted me to come here. So I kept on my way. But I must admit, my feet moved slower and slower upon the path.

It was nearly sundown when I approached a huge, dark building in the middle of a valley. The country all around it was pleasant, but the house itself appeared to be a ruin. No smoke rose from the chimneys, nor was there any light. The closer I got, the worse the building looked. Parts of it seemed to never have been finished, and the whole thing looked shabby and uncared for.

I walked slowly up to the door and knocked. I could hear movement inside, but no one came to let me in. Then I grew angry, and began to pound and kick at the door, calling on Ebenezer Balfour to come out.

I heard a noise above me, and looked up to see a man's head peering out of a window at me. He was holding a gun. "This is loaded," he threatened.

"I have come with a letter for Mr. Ebenezer Balfour," I said.

"Put it on the doorstep and be gone."

I was getting angrier by the minute at this rude treatment. "I will do no such thing!" I shouted. "This is a letter of introduction, and I mean to give it to Mr. Balfour myself."

"Who are you?"

"I am David Balfour."

8

My answer must have startled the old man, for the gun shook in his hands. For a moment, he said nothing. Then, "Is your father dead?" He did not wait for me to answer. "Yes, of course he is. That's why you're here. All right. I'll let you in."

The door was opened with a great rattling of chains and bolts. The man slammed it behind me as soon as I entered. We went into the kitchen. "Let me see the letter," he demanded.

"It is for Mr. Balfour, not for you," I told him, still angry.

"And who do you think I am?" said the man, just as furious as I was. "I am Ebenezer Balfour, and your father was my brother! I'm your uncle, Davie, lad. Now, give me the letter."

I could think of nothing to say, so I handed him the letter without a word. He seemed pleased after he'd read it.

"We'll get along just fine, you and me," he said. "Now, come up to bed. We'll have plenty of time to get to know one another in the morning."

In the days that followed, my uncle and I did get to know each other, but things were not very friendly between us. My uncle was a very strange man. He would have nothing to do with other folk, and he often fell into fits of angry shouting that frightened me. But, at other times, he would go out of his way to be nice to me, saying that we were related, and families should stick together. When I offered to leave his home after one argument, he all but begged me to stay. "I'll do right by you, Davie," he promised me. "I'll do right, you'll see."

One night, he said to me, "There are some papers you should see, Davie. They're in a chest in the tower at the far end of the house. Run along and fetch them for me."

"Can I have a light?" I asked, for the night was very dark.

"No," he said, "you'll do fine without one. The stairs are sturdy. Go along."

I went out into the night. The wind was moaning, and I could feel a bad storm coming. In fact, I had just reached the tower when a great bolt of lightning split the sky.

I made my way carefully into the tower, moving slowly in the darkness. I laid one hand against the wall to steady myself as I moved up and up the long flight of stairs.

Then, a great flash of lightning lit up everything around me and revealed a scene so horrible that I was too frightened to even scream. There were great holes in the wall that let in the light, and no railings on the staircase. The steps were uneven in length, and one wrong move would send me tumbling down into darkness. In fact, at that very moment, my foot was barely two inches from the edge!

10

I realized that my uncle meant to kill me, and an angry courage filled me. I got down on my hands and knees and made my way carefully back down the stairs. The storm raged all around me, the tower shaking in the wind and torrents of rain coming through the walls to drench my clothes.

When I crept back into the kitchen, my uncle was sitting with his back to me. I slipped behind him as quietly as I could, then suddenly clapped my hands down on his shoulders. "Ah!" I shouted.

My uncle gave a terrible cry, flung up his hands, and fell to the floor in a dead faint.

I had not expected that, but I took his keys and his knife from him as he lay there. When my uncle began to stir, I helped him sit up. Then I demanded an explanation from him.

"I'll tell you in the morning," he said. I hated to wait, but he was so weak and shaken that I had no choice. So, I locked the old man in his room and went to bed, feeling that I had gotten the better of my uncle at last.

I never did get my explanation. As we were eating breakfast the next morning, a knock came at the door. I went to answer it, and found a young boy waiting there. He was a strange lad, dressed in ragged clothes. He had a look about him as if he did not know whether to laugh or cry. And when I asked what he wanted, he began to sing an old song.

It took some time, but I finally got out of him that he had a letter for my uncle, from a ship's captain named Hoseason in the town of Queensferry.

"I have some business with this captain, Davie," my uncle told me. "Why don't you and I go into town together? After I finish talking to Hoseason, I'll take you to see a lawyer named Mr. Rankeillor. He knew your father, and he'll explain your inheritance to you."

I was wary of my uncle, but I thought that in the midst of a great crowd of people in town, he could do me no harm. And I was interested to see the ship and the sea.

So, we walked into town. Uncle Ebenezer went a little ahead, while I walked with the strange boy. He was a cabin boy on Hoseason's ship, and his name was Ransome.

I waited outside an office building while my uncle and Hoseason had their meeting. Afterwards, the captain said to me, "Your uncle says you are from a place far from the sea and have never been on a ship. How would you both like to come on board my ship, the *Covenant,* for a little while?"

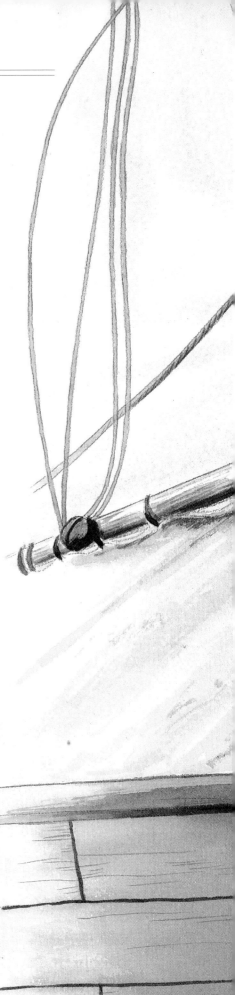

I longed to see the inside of a ship more than words can tell, but I still did not trust my uncle. I told the captain that we had an appointment with a lawyer and could not be late.

"Aye," Hoseason said, "your uncle spoke of that. I can sail you down to the pier. Mr. Rankeillor's house is nearby." And with that, he slipped an arm through my own and began to walk toward the harbor, talking about the sea all the while.

Hoseason seemed like such a friendly and trustworthy man, and I was so eager to go on board a ship, that I forgot my worries altogether. The captain, my uncle, and I boarded a small rowboat and set off over the water.

When we reached the *Covenant,* the captain swung me over the rail and then climbed up to stand beside me on the deck. I was a little dizzy with the unsteadiness of the boat, and a little afraid, too. But I was very pleased to be there.

Then I realized Hoseason and I were alone on the deck. "Where is my uncle?" I cried.

Hoseason's face was suddenly grim and cold. "That's the point," he said.

I pulled away from him and ran to the rail. Sure enough, there was the rowboat pulling away from the ship, with my uncle sitting in the stern. He turned toward me with a cruel expression on his face.

That was the last thing I saw. Strong hands pulled me back from the ship's side. Then a thunderbolt seemed to strike me. I saw a great flash of fire, and I fell senseless.

I woke in darkness, in great pain, and bound hand and foot. Everything around me seemed to be plunging up and down. It took me some time to realize I must be lying somewhere deep inside the *Covenant*. That thought filled me with a great despair and anger.

Day and night were alike in that horrid cavern, and my misery seemed to double the hours. I do not know how long I lay there before I saw a light approaching. Then a lantern shone in my face and I saw a man looking down at me. "How goes it?" he asked.

I was so miserable that the only answer I could give him was a sob. At that, he sat down and began to wash and dress the wound on my head. He gave me something to drink before he left me alone again.

The next time he came to see me, I was very ill with dizziness and fever, and I was in great pain besides. This time, the man brought the captain with him. He told Hoseason I would die if I had no light and fresh air, and the captain agreed. My friend untied me and carried me up to a comfortable bunk. There I lay sleeping for a long time.

In the days that followed, I came to know my companions. They were a rough lot, but then, they had a rough life, so that could not be helped. And they were kind to me in their way, especially Mr. Riach, the mate who had brought me from below deck.

I found out where the ship was bound, and that knowledge filled me with despair again. For we were headed to the Carolinas. In those days, men were still sold into slavery to work in the fields of the plantations there. That was the fate that lay ahead of me.

One of my chief companions on the ship was Ransome, the young cabin boy. He was a sad creature, for his master, a mate named Mr. Shuan, often beat him. I felt sorry for the lad.

Then, one black night, Captain Hoseason came to find me. "You are to have Ransome's place now," he said. "Go up to the roundhouse where Mr. Shuan, Mr. Riach, and I live, and do what you're told."

At that same moment, two men appeared, carrying Ransome in their arms. His face was white as wax. I knew then that Mr. Shuan had finally gone too far and had killed the boy.

"Go!" ordered Hoseason, and I ran up on deck.

I should have hated Mr. Shuan for his cruelty, but I soon realized he was not quite right in his mind. As I went about my new duties serving the captain and the two mates, I found myself pitying him instead. The work in the roundhouse kept me busy, but I was glad of that. It kept me from thinking about the fate ahead of me.

About ten days after I came to the roundhouse, the *Covenant* sailed into a heavy fog. We moved slowly through the water, unable to see a thing. About ten that night, while I was serving Mr. Riach and Hoseason their supper, there was a great crash and a lot of shouting. ''She's struck something!'' Mr. Riach cried.

It turned out we had run down a smaller boat in the fog. That unlucky ship split in two and sank. Only one man survived, and Hoseason brought him on board the *Covenant*.

He was a young man, very elegantly dressed, with a sword, a pair of pistols, and a pouch of gold on his belt. Hoseason seemed to stare overlong at that pouch of gold.

The stranger's name was Alan Breck. He wanted Hoseason to ferry him to France, where he had been heading when we struck his ship. But Hoseason said this was too far out of his way. Finally, the two agreed on a price to bring Alan back to Scotland.

The captain left the roundhouse, while I stayed behind to fix supper for Alan. We chatted quite merrily together, and I decided I liked this well-dressed stranger. After a time, he asked me to fetch him something to drink. As the captain had the key to the storeroom, I went in search of him.

I found Hoseason, Mr. Riach, and Mr. Shuan with their heads together, and I knew, even before I came close enough to hear them, that they were up to no good. And, indeed, they were. They were talking of murdering Alan Breck and stealing his money!

I decided to pretend I agreed with this plan. So, when they asked me to fetch them their pistols from the roundhouse, I said yes.

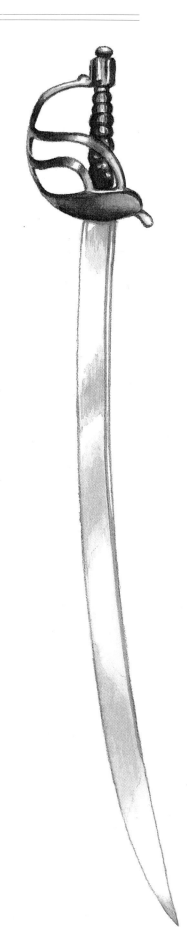

I went back to the roundhouse with my thoughts all in a whirl. What was I to do? These men had stolen me from my country and killed poor Ransome, and now they planned to commit another murder. But how could I stop them? I was just a boy, and I had too much fear of death to go against a whole ship's company.

Then I walked into the roundhouse and looked at Alan, calmly eating his supper, and my mind was made up in an instant. I put my hand on the stranger's shoulder. ''Do you want to be killed?'' I asked him.

Alan jumped to his feet and stared at me. ''They're all murderers here,'' I told him. ''It's a ship full of them! They've murdered a boy already, and now they plan to murder you.''

''They haven't gotten me yet,'' Alan said. ''Will you stand by me, David?''

''That I will,'' I said, ''for I am no thief or murderer.''

So, we made our plans. I figured we had fifteen men against us, but the roundhouse was very strong and should make a good fortress. Alan set himself to guard one of the doors with his sword, while I took his two pistols and watched the other door and the windows.

We had scarcely gotten into position when the sailors realized I was not going to bring them their guns and attacked us. I do not know if I was what you call afraid, but my heart beat as fast as a bird's. I had no hope. I only wished for the battle to be over as soon as possible.

I had a glimpse of Alan crossing swords with Mr. Shuan. ''That's the man who killed the boy!'' I shouted to him.

''Look to your windows,'' Alan told me, and ran his sword through Mr. Shuan's body.

I turned to see five men coming toward the roundhouse with a battering ram. I had never fired a pistol in my life, but I raised the guns and shot into their midst. I do not know whether I hit anyone or not, but the men scattered and fled at the shots.

Then there came a great shattering of glass, and a man leaped through the windows and into the room. I clapped my pistol to his back and prepared to shoot him—but I could not do it.

The man turned and shouted at me, grabbing my shirt. I was afraid he would kill me. I knew I had no choice but to shoot him, so I did. He fell to the floor with a terrible groan, and I stood staring at him.

I might have stood there forever if I had not heard Alan shouting for help. He had been holding the door alone, but now a man was trying to wrestle him to the ground, as more men burst through the door. I ran toward the mob with my pistols raised. Just then, Alan pulled free of his opponent and thrust forward with his sword. At the sight of us, the group turned and ran. At last we heard them tumble down the ladder below deck. Then it was very quiet.

Alan threw his arms around me in triumph. "David, you are like a brother to me," he said. But there was a tightness in my chest that made it hard to breathe, and the thought of the man I had killed weighed on me like a nightmare. Before I realized what was happening, I was sobbing like a child.

Alan patted my shoulder. "You're a brave lad," he told me. "You just need to get some sleep. I'll take first watch so you can rest."

The night passed uneventfully, and Alan and I sat down to breakfast about six o'clock the next morning. We made good company for each other. At one point, Alan took a knife from the table, cut off one of the silver buttons on his coat, and gave it to me.

"I got these from my father," he said, "and I want you to keep one for last night's work. Wherever you go and show this button, the friends of Alan Breck will help you."

After a time, we heard Mr. Riach calling us. Alan and I went out on deck with our weapons drawn and sat at some distance from Mr. Riach and the captain to discuss what we would do now. It was agreed that Hoseason would sail the ship back to Glasgow, in Scotland. There he could get some men to replace his dead and injured crew, and Alan and I could depart in safety.

As soon as a wind came up, we set out, making our way along the coast of Scotland. After the horrors I had seen, it seemed like an uneventful journey—but the adventure was far from over.

One evening, Hoseason called to Alan and me to come out on deck. He seemed very worried. The wind was blowing hard, but the sky was clear. It was not a bad night for sailing, and I wondered why the captain was so concerned. Then I heard a low, roaring sound and saw the sea rise like a fountain in several places around us.

"They're reefs," Alan said.

"Aye," Hoseason agreed, "and if I'd known they were here, I'd never have sailed into them."

"These are the Torran Rocks," Alan said. "I believe I've heard it is clearer along the land."

"Then that's where we shall sail. Will you stay and help me pilot us through them?"

Alan agreed, and the two of us took our places by the captain. The moon shone down as bright as day, which made the sight of our danger all the more alarming. The captain paced nervously about the deck, and Alan was very pale. "This is not the sort of death I fancy," he said to me.

The tide was strong along the land, and it was all the men could do to keep the *Covenant* on her course. Sometimes, a reef would loom up in our very path, and the ship would barely be turned in time.

We made our way slowly through the reefs and, finally, caught sight of clear water ahead. "You have saved the ship," Hoseason said to Alan. But he spoke too soon.

The tide caught the boat and pushed her around into the wind. She spun around like a top, and the next moment struck a reef with such force that we were all thrown flat on the deck.

I was on my feet in a minute. The waves broke high over the ship, sweeping over the deck. We could hear the ship grinding against the reef. It seemed she would soon break into pieces.

I ran over to help the men untie one of the small rowboats that lay on the deck. We had the boat nearly ready to be launched when someone shouted, "Hold on!" in a voice full of terror.

A great wave lifted the ship straight up and tipped her sideways. Whether the cry was too late or my grip too weak, I do not know. The sudden tilting of the ship threw me clean over the rail and into the sea.

I went down, choking on sea water, then came up into the moonlight, only to plunge under the water once more. I lost count of how many times I went down and came up again. All the while, I was being hurled along, with the water beating upon me and choking me. I scarcely knew what was happening.

Presently, I found I was holding onto a piece of wood, and that I was in quieter water. The brig was far away from me now, much too far to reach, for I was no great swimmer. Land was closer. I held tight to the length of wood and kicked as strongly as I could toward the coast. After about an hour of kicking and splashing, I felt dry land under my feet. I dragged myself up onto the beach.

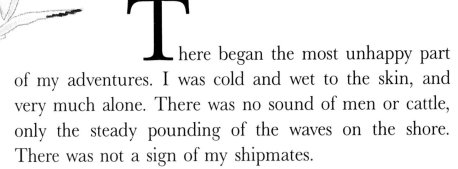

There began the most unhappy part of my adventures. I was cold and wet to the skin, and very much alone. There was no sound of men or cattle, only the steady pounding of the waves on the shore. There was not a sign of my shipmates.

When morning broke, I began to walk along, thinking to come to a house where I might warm myself and get news of those I had lost. It was the roughest kind of walking, for the land was nothing but a jumble of rocks and heather.

Soon I came to a creek that was too wide and too deep for me to cross. I changed my course to walk along the banks of it, thinking it would soon narrow enough for me to get across. But it did not. It wasn't until I came upon a rise of ground that allowed me to look all around that I realized where I was. I had been set upon a barren island, cut off on every side by the sea, and there was no one here to help me.

The days that followed are bitter to recall. I had nothing to eat but the shellfish I found among the rocks of my island, which often made me ill, and nothing to drink but rainwater I scooped out of puddles. My situation was made all the more unbearable by the sight of smoke rising from the chimneys of the houses on an island nearby—an island I could not reach.

It seemed impossible that I should be left to die within sight of a town. But, as a second day passed, and most of a third, without any boat coming close enough to call to, it seemed that my life would, indeed, end there.

It was on the third day that a small fishing boat suddenly passed close to the island. I shouted out to the two men on board, for they were close enough to hear—I could even see the color of their hair. There was no doubt that they saw me, for they called out and laughed. But the boat never turned, never slowed down. Indeed, they sailed past my very eyes and disappeared over the horizon.

I could not believe such wickedness. I ran along the shore from rock to rock, calling after them, even though they were long out of my sight. I thought my heart would burst with disappointment.

The next day, the fourth of this horrible life, I found my strength very low, and my spirits, too. I had no sooner finished my breakfast of shellfish and climbed onto a rock to watch the sea when I saw a boat coming in my direction.

I soon realized it was the same boat I had seen yesterday, and I thought perhaps the fishermen had thought better of their cruelty to me and were coming to my rescue. But, although the boat came quite close to the shore, it did not draw near enough for me to climb aboard. What frightened me most of all was that the men were laughing at me.

Finally, one man stood up and began to talk to me, but he spoke a language I could not understand. I was able to make out a few words, though. One word I caught was ''tide,'' spoken as the man waved his hand toward the main island nearby.

All at once, I understood what he was trying to tell me. ''Do you mean when the tide is out—'' I cried, but could not finish.

''Yes, yes!'' the man shouted, laughing even harder now.

I turned away and ran toward the creek. Sure enough, it had shrunk into a little trickle of water which barely rose above my knees as I dashed across. I threw myself down on the main island with a shout.

A sea-bred boy would not have stayed a day on my island, for it was what is called a tidal islet. Twice a day, when the tide went out, it was simple to cross to the main island. But I had not known that, and so I had suffered terribly for four long and lonely days. I felt like a perfect fool. No wonder the fishermen had laughed at me so!

I was now on an island called the Ross of Mull. It was as rugged as the place I had left, but at least there were people here. I set out in the direction of the smoke I had seen while I was shipwrecked.

About five or six that night, I came to a long, low house tucked into a valley. An old man sat smoking his pipe in front of it. He told me that one of my shipmates had been in that very house the day after the *Covenant* went to her watery grave.

"Was he dressed like a gentleman?" I asked.

"Indeed, he was," the man said, and I knew his guest had been my friend Alan. This news set me smiling.

"Why, you must be the lad with the silver button!" the man cried. I told him I was, and he went on. "Your friend left word for you. He says you are to follow him to his part of the country, called Appin, by way of Torosay."

This man was very kind to me, for he brought me inside and fed me a hearty meal. Then he told me I was welcome to sleep there for the night, so I would be well-rested to start my journey the next morning.

I walked the fifty miles to Torosay in four days. In Torosay, I received word to take a ferry to Kinlochaline on the mainland.

The ferryman's name was Neil Roy Macrob. Alan had told me that Macrob was the name of one of his clansmen, so I was eager to talk to Neil Roy in private. This was impossible on the crowded boat, but once we reached Kinlochaline, I drew him aside and showed him the button Alan had given to me.

Neil Roy gave me a complicated series of instructions that would finally lead me to the house of Alan's cousin, James of the Glens. I could not take a straight course because there was trouble between Alan's clan and an important gentleman named Colin Roy Campbell of Glenure. It seemed the English soldiers were watching for Alan.

As I drew closer to Appin, I realized Neil Roy had been right. I caught sight of soldiers everywhere along the road. This made me very uneasy. I was not so sure I wanted to join Alan after all, if he was in such serious trouble as this.

As I was sitting beside the road and thinking of what I should do, I heard the sound of men and horses coming through the woods toward me. Soon four men came into view, leading their horses along the rough and narrow path. The first man was a gentleman, to be sure, from the way he was dressed.

On seeing the group, I decided to go on with my adventure, though I am not sure why. I stood up and asked the gentleman if he knew the way to Aucharn, the place where James of the Glens lived.

The men spoke together, and I heard the gentleman called by name. It was then that I realized who I had stopped. It was none other than Colin Roy Campbell of Glenure—Alan's enemy!

As we stood talking, a shot suddenly rang out from higher up the hill. The gentleman fell onto the road. "Oh, I am dead!" he cried as his friend hurried to take him into his arms.

I could do no more than stare at them in horror. It was not until Glenure's friend laid his body down in the road that I came to my senses and ran up the hill.

I could see the man who had fired the shot moving up the mountain some distance ahead of me. He was a big man in a black coat. I had only a glimpse of him before he disappeared into a grove of birch trees.

"There's a reward if you take the lad!" shouted Glenure's friend as a group of soldiers hurried down the road. I knew he was talking about me. "He was in on the plot, and stopped us so the murderer could take his aim!"

At that, I was filled with a new kind of terror. I was so frightened and amazed at this sudden turn of events that I scarcely knew what to do. Then, "Duck in here among the trees," said a voice close by.

I did so, and found Alan Breck standing there with a fishing rod over his shoulder. He gave me no greeting— indeed, there was no time for that. "Come!" was all he said before he started running along the side of the mountain. Not knowing what else to do, I followed him.

For a quarter of an hour, we ran through the trees or crawled through the heather. Our pace was deadly. My heart felt like it would burst against my ribs and I had no breath to speak with.

Every so often, Alan would stop and move to stand where the soldiers could see him. Each time he did this, there came a great shout from behind us. Then we would run again.

Finally, when I thought I could not take another step, Alan stopped and lay flat in the heather. I dropped down beside him and we both lay panting and gasping for breath.

After a time, Alan rose and looked past the border of the trees, then came back and sat beside me. "Well," he said, "that was a fast race, David."

I said nothing. I could not even lift my head. I had seen a murder, a great man struck down in a moment, but that was only part of my distress. A man Alan hated had been killed, and here was Alan hiding in the trees and running from the soldiers. I knew he had not fired the shot, but if he had ordered the death, he was just as guilty. I could not look at him. In fact, I would rather have been alone in the rain on my cold island than be there in the woods beside a murderer.

"Are you so tired?" Alan asked me.

"No," I said, with my face still pressed into the heather, "but I fear I can follow you no longer. I liked you very much, Alan, but your ways are not my ways, and I cannot stay with you a moment more."

"Why? It is only fair that you tell me what I've done to upset you."

"You know very well what it is!" I cried. "There is a man lying dead on the road!"

"And you think I had a hand in it. You're jumping to conclusions, David Balfour."

"Are you saying you didn't?" I asked, sitting up.

"Mr. Balfour," said Alan, "if I were going to kill a gentleman, I would not do it in my own part of the country, to bring trouble on my clan. And I would not do it with a fishing rod on my back rather than a sword or a gun!"

"That's true," I had to admit.

Alan took out his knife and laid his hand upon it. "I swear to you that I had no part in the murder."

"All right, then." A new thought came to me. "Do you know who did it?" I asked. "He must have run right by you in the woods."

"Well," Alan said with a smile, "he *did* run close by me, but by an odd coincidence, I had just bent to tie my shoes at that very moment."

"Can you swear that you don't know him?" I asked, half angry and half laughing.

"Not yet," he said, "but I've a grand memory for forgetting, David."

"You did show yourself to draw the soldiers after us."

"Any gentleman would do the same," Alan said sternly.

He humbled me with that, and we spoke no more about it.

But we had no sooner settled that matter than we had a disagreement about another. I was all for turning ourselves in and clearing our names. "I have no fear of justice in my own country," I said grandly.

"David, I wonder about you!" Alan exclaimed. "This is an important man who has been killed. The case will be tried in his home town, with all his friends in the jury box. Justice? We'd have the same justice as Glenure found a while ago at the roadside."

That frightened me, I confess. Alan went on. "When I tell you to run, take my word and run. It may be a hard thing to hide in the heather, but it's harder yet to lie chained in prison." Then he said we could flee in the direction of Queensferry, which is where I wanted very much to go.

"All right, Alan," I said at last, "I'll go with you."

"Mind you," he said, "this is no small thing. You will lie cold and wet and be hungry more than once before we're done. Your life shall be like the hunted deer, and you will sleep with your hand upon your weapons. I tell you this at the start, for it's a life I know well. But if you ask what other chance you have, I tell you, none. Either take to the heather with me or hang."

"That's a choice that's easily made," I said, and we shook hands on it.

We looked out between the trees and saw that the soldiers were very far away. Alan said we had time to rest and eat before we set out for Aucharn and the home of his kinsman, James of the Glens. There we could get clothes and weapons and money. "And then," said Alan, "we'll take our chances in the heather!"

ight fell as we walked, and it was about half past ten before we came to the top of a hill and saw lights below us. Firelight streamed from the open door of a house, and five or six persons were moving around the yard in a great hurry, each carrying a torch.

"James must have lost his wits," Alan said. "If it were the soldiers instead of us, he'd be in great trouble." Then, he whistled three times, in a special signal. At the sound, everyone stopped for a moment. Then they went back to their work as we started down the hill.

A tall man met us at the gate. This was Alan's cousin, James of the Glens. He seemed very upset. "There has been a terrible accident," he cried to Alan. "It will bring trouble on us all!"

"You must take the sour with the sweet," Alan told him. "Glenure is dead."

"I wish he were alive again! It's all very fine to boast about such a thing beforehand, but now that it's done, it's the people of this area that must pay for it. I worry about my family."

Indeed, the man was so frightened that he would not even give us much help. He gave me a change of clothes and both of us some weapons. But as for money, which we were in sore need of, there was none to spare.

There was no time for us to waste staying there, and we were a danger to James's family besides. "Tomorrow there will be a fine to-do in Appin," Alan said, "a fine display of soldiers. It is best for us to be gone, and the sooner the better." And so, we said good-bye and set out again over much the same rugged country as before.

Sometimes we walked, sometimes we ran, and as morning drew closer, we walked less and ran more. But for all our hurry, day began while we were still far from any shelter. At last we found ourselves by two great rocks leaning together near a river. It took us several tries to climb them, they were that high. But once we reached the top, I knew why Alan had come there. There was a kind of saucer at the top, where as many as three or four men could lay hidden.

We settled into our hiding place, and Alan bid me to sleep while he took the first watch. I was sound asleep almost before I knew it.

It was late in the morning when Alan woke me, complaining that I had been snoring. "Look," he said grimly.

About half a mile up the river was a camp of soldiers. Sentries were posted all along the bank, perched on rocks much like ours. I took but one look and dove back into our hiding place.

"This is what I was afraid of, Davie," Alan said. "We're in trouble. If they go up the sides of the hill, they'll easily spot us. We can only hope they'll stay in the valley until nightfall. Then we'll have a chance of getting by them."

So we spent the day lying on that rock, and an uncomfortable day it was! It was very hot, and the sun beat down on us cruelly. The rock grew so hot we could barely stand the touch of it. There was a little patch of ferns that was cooler, but it was only large enough for one person at a time. We took turns lying there to get a bit of relief.

The soldiers kept stirring all day, and sometimes they came so close to our rock that we scarcely dared breathe. And all the while, the rock grew hotter and the sun fiercer, until I felt dizzy and sick.

At last, about two in the afternoon, there came a patch of shade on one side of the rock. It was the side nearest to the soldiers' camp, but by that time Alan and I were past caring, we were so miserable and ill from the sun. We dropped down into the shadow and laid there for several hours, as weak as water, and quite easy to spot by any soldier who came near. None came, however, which was very lucky for us!

After a time, we got our strength back. The soldiers had moved closer to the riverside, so Alan suggested we try to make our escape. By this time, I was afraid of nothing save for having to climb onto that rock once more, so I agreed.

We got ourselves ready and began to slip from rock to rock, one after the other, now crawling flat on our bellies, now making a run for it, all the while with our hearts in our mouths. It was the most tiring and frightening thing I have ever taken part in, for the slightest sound or movement could give us away and bring the whole troop of soldiers down around us.

By sundown, we had made some distance toward the mountains. Once night fell and the moon rose to light our way, we were able to move more quickly. Our path was a tricky one, lying as it did along the steep sides of mountains and along the edges of cliffs. I was in terrible fear of falling the entire time.

We traveled in this manner for more days than I can count, hiding in the heather by day, walking for miles at night. Sometimes we came across a friend of Alan who would hide us in his house for a day or two, and feed us a proper meal. In this manner, we made our way across mountains, woods, and heather, until at last we reached Queensferry, where my uncle and Mr. Rankeillor, the lawyer, lived.

It was now late in the month of August, more than two months since I had been there last. I was more eager than ever to get the better of my uncle and set my affairs straight. Alan and I agreed that he would hide himself in the woods outside of Queensferry while I went into town to find Mr. Rankeillor. We arranged to meet in a field at nightfall.

I was in the main street of Queensferry before dawn. But as the morning grew later and people began to go about their business, I found I could not ask where Mr. Rankeillor lived. I was so shabbily dressed and worn out from my long adventure that I was ashamed to ask for the house of such a fine man as Mr. Rankeillor. I thought that whoever I asked would laugh in my face. So I went up and down the street, down to the harbor and back again, like a dog that has lost its master.

At last, I was so tired from all this walking that I stopped to rest in front of a very fancy house. As I was sitting there, a gentleman came out of the house and caught sight of me. I was in such a pitiful state that he must have felt sorry for me. He came up beside me and asked me why I was there.

I told him I had come to Queensferry on business. Then, taking heart at his kind face, I asked him the way to Mr. Rankeillor's house.

"Why," he said, "this is his house right here, and I am that very man! But I do not know your name or your face."

"My name is David Balfour," I told him, and the look on his face changed to one of complete surprise. "I have come from a great many strange places, but I think it would be better to tell you all about them somewhere more private."

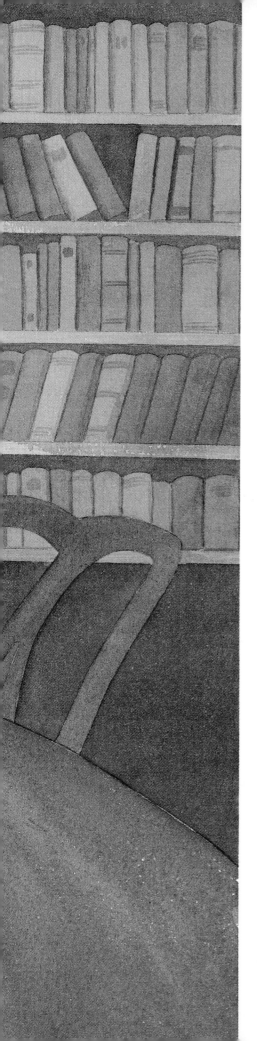

Mr. Rankeillor agreed, and led me into his house. We settled into a dusty room full of books and papers, and there I told him all of my story, from my arrival at my uncle's house and his cruel betrayal of me, to the shipwreck and my flight across the heather with Alan.

"Your friend, Mr. Campbell from Essendean, came asking about you," Mr. Rankeillor said. "Your uncle told him he had given you a large amount of money and you had gone off to Europe. Nobody believed him, including me. In fact, your uncle and I had such a fight about it that I am no longer working for him."

That was a relief to me. Although I knew Mr. Rankeillor was my only hope, I was unsure how close he was to my uncle.

"Then the captain of the ship you sailed on came back to town," Mr. Rankeillor went on. "He said that the ship had sunk and you had drowned, along with many other men."

Our conversation then turned to my inheritance. My father's estate was mine beyond a doubt according to the law. "Still," Mr. Rankeillor said, "your uncle is a very selfish man. He will fight you over this. He might even bring a lawsuit against you. If that happened, not only would all your business be brought out for the public to see, but your friend would also be involved, since you have spent the better part of two months in his company. If you can get your uncle to admit to the kidnapping, then you can make a bargain with him. Let him keep his house, for he has lived there for twenty-five years. But make it clear that you will tell everyone he had you kidnapped unless he gives you your fair share of the money."

I told him I was very willing to do this. Then we came up with a plan to accomplish what we wished.

As dusk came, Mr. Rankeillor and I set out for the place where Alan was waiting. Mr. Rankeillor's clerk, Torrance, was also with us. He would be a witness to all that happened that evening.

I went ahead to tell Alan of our plan. He was to play a large part in it, which pleased him greatly. I then introduced him to the other two, and we all set out for my uncle's house.

Night had fallen by the time we reached Shaws. All of us but Alan crouched down beside a corner of the house, well hidden. Alan himself walked boldly up to the door and began to knock.

It was some time before my uncle came to the window to see what all the noise was about. "What brings you here?" he demanded, pointing a gun at Alan.

"David," Alan said simply.

"What was that?" said my uncle in a very different voice. Then, "I'd better ask you in."

"Yes," said Alan, "but the question is, would I go? I think we should have our discussion right here on the doorstep."

"All right," the old man agreed, and presently he came down. The gun was still in his hands.

Alan began the tale we had devised. "I have friends on the Isle of Mull. It seems a ship was lost in those parts, and the next day, one of my friends found a lad half-drowned on the beach. Now, my friends aren't too fond of the law, and they've shut the boy up in a castle. They've asked me to call on you, Mr. Balfour, and see how much money you'll give them if you want to see the boy again."

My uncle cleared his throat. "I don't care much for him," he said. "He's not a good lad, and I'll pay no ransom for him."

"You cannot desert your own nephew like that! If the folk in this town came to know of it, you wouldn't be very popular."

"I'm not very popular now," replied my uncle. "Anyway, how would they find out? I wouldn't speak of it, and I don't see why you should."

"Then it will have to be David that tells it," said Alan.

"How's that?" my uncle asked sharply.

"Well," said Alan, "if my friends were to know they'd get no money for the lad, they would probably let him go where he pleased. It seems to me that either you like David and would pay to have him back, or you don't like him and would pay us to keep him. Now, if you don't want him back, as it seems you don't, what do you want done with him and how much will you pay us to do it?"

My uncle was silent for so long that Alan finally spoke again. "Do you want the lad killed or kept?" he asked with a touch of impatience.

At that, my uncle looked frightened. "Oh, kept! I'll have no bloodshed, if you please."

"Well," said Alan, "keeping the lad will cost you more. It's not so easy for me to set a price. I'd have to know first what you paid Hoseason for kidnapping David in the first place."

"Kidnapping!" my uncle cried. "Did David tell you that? If he did, he lied!"

"It wasn't David, Mr. Balfour. It was Hoseason. You know," Alan continued calmly, "Hoseason's not the sort of man I would let in on a secret like that. He told me all about your plans. Now, sir, what did you pay him?"

"Twenty pounds," my uncle admitted, "plus whatever he got for selling the lad in the Carolinas."

"Thank you, Alan, you've done very well," said Mr. Rankeillor as he stepped out of the shadows. "Good evening, Mr. Balfour."

And, "Good evening, Uncle Ebenezer," I said.

And, "It's a lovely night, isn't it, Mr. Balfour?" added Torrance.

My uncle never said a word. He just sat there and stared like a man turned to stone. Alan plucked his gun away as easy as you please, and Mr. Rankeillor led him into the kitchen, with the rest of us following behind.

My affairs were settled that very night. I would have two thirds of the income from my estate, and my uncle would keep the house and land.

As for Alan, who had been such a help to me in all of this, Mr. Rankeillor gave us excellent advice on what to do. There was a lawyer in the city of Edinburgh who was from Appin, and who was sympathetic to Alan's plight. Mr. Rankeillor placed money in my name in a bank in Edinburgh. With this money, the lawyer would arrange for Alan's safe escape to France.

Edinburgh, then, was the place where Alan and I said our good-byes. We were both very downhearted that day. The memory of all the adventures we had shared weighed upon us heavily. We tried to joke, but we both knew we were closer to tears than to laughter.

''Well, good-bye,'' Alan said at last, holding out a hand.

''Good-bye,'' I said, and gave his hand a shake. Then, I hurried down the hill.

Neither of us looked back at the other. But once I was alone, I felt so lost and lonesome that I could have sat down by the road and cried like a child.

I wandered through the streets of Edinburgh, stunned at the height of the buildings, the throngs of people, and all the other sights and sounds of a great city. I let the crowd carry me to and fro, thinking sadly of Alan all the while.

At last, I found the bank where Mr. Rankeillor had placed my money, and I went inside to begin my new life.